NURSE MATILDA

Once upon a time there was a huge family of children, and they were terribly, terribly naughty.

Not a week passed by but one of the staff gave notice and had to be replaced. Till the day came when they all gave notice together –
'Mr and Mrs Brown, your children are so naughty that we can't stand it one minute longer.

Miss Tora has cut off one of Miss Susie's plaits – and Master David has made a beard out of it, and glued it on to Miss Charlotte.
Miss Helen has poured syrup into all the wellington boots –
Miss Stephanie has grated up soap to look like cheese, and now poor Cook's dinner does nothing but foam –
– and all the other children are doing simply dreadful things too . . .'

The answer to the Browns' prayers arrives – as if by magic: Nurse Matilda!

·♫ Nurse Matilda ♫·

Nurse Matilda

Christianna Brand

Illustrated by
Edward Ardizzone

KNIGHT BOOKS
Hodder and Stoughton

**To Tora –
And to our Hilde,
with love**

Text copyright © 1964 by Christianna Brand
Illustrations copyright © 1964 by Edward Ardizzone

First published in Great Britain in 1964 by Brockhampton Press, now Hodder & Stoughton Children's Books

This edition first published by Knight Books 1973

This impression 1991

Printed and bound in Great Britain for Hodder and Stoughton Children's Books, a division of Hodder and Stoughton Ltd., Mill Road, Dunton Green, Sevenoaks, Kent TN13 2YA. (Editorial Office: 47 Bedford Square, London WC1B 3DP) by Cox & Wyman Ltd., Reading, Berks.

British Libary C.I.P.

A C.I.P. catalogue record of this book is available from the British Library

ISBN 0 340 17462 5

Chapter 1

NCE upon a time there was a huge family of children; and they were terribly, terribly naughty.

In those days, mothers and fathers used to have much larger families than they do now; and these large families often *were* naughty. The mothers and fathers had to have all sorts of nurses and nannies and governesses (who were often French or German) to look after all their naughty children: and usually one poor, skinny little nursery-maid to wait on all the nurses and governesses and nannies . . .

This family I'm telling you about seemed to have more children, and naughtier children, than any other. There were so many of them that I shan't even tell you their names but leave you to sort them out as you go along, and add up how many there were. But even their parents had to think of them in groups – there were the Big Ones and the Middling Ones and the Little Ones and the Littlest Ones; and the Baby. The baby was really a splendid character. It had fat, bent legs and its nappy was always falling down round its fat, pink knees; but it kept up with the children to the last ounce of its strength. It talked a curious language all of its own.

There was also the Tiny Baby, but it was so small that it *couldn't* be naughty, so it was very dull and we needn't count it.

The children had two dogs, who were dachshunds. One was a goldeny brown and he was called Brown Sugar or Barley Sugar or sometimes even Demerara Sugar, but anyway, Sugar for short. The other was tiny and black and as sleek as a little seal and she was called Spice.

And the naughtiness of these children was almost past believing. Not a week passed by but the fat nanny or one of the two starchy nurses or the French governess or the skinny little nursery-maid gave notice and had to be replaced by a new fat nanny or starchy nurse or foreign governess or skinny little nursery-maid. Till a day came when they all gave notice together, rising up in a body and marching into the drawing-room and saying with one voice, 'Mr and Mrs Brown' – for that was the name of the children's father and mother – 'your children are so naughty that we can't stand it one minute longer and we're all going away.'

Mrs Brown was very sweet and she never could believe that her children were really naughty. She opened her eyes very wide and said, 'Oh, dear, what have they been doing now?'

So they all began:

'*Miss Tora has cut off one of Miss Susie's plaits*—'

'*— and Master David has made a beard out of it, and glued it on to Miss Charlotte.*'

'*Master Simon 'ave dress up ze dachshoooond in my best Parees 'at, and take eem for ze promenade.*'

'*Miss Helen has poured syrup into all the Wellington boots*—'

'*Miss Stephanie has grated up soap to look like cheese, and now poor Cook's dinner does nothing but foam*—'

'*— and all the other children are doing simply dreadful things too . . .*'

'What *you* need,' they added, speaking in unison, 'is Nurse Matilda.' And they all turned and marched out of the drawing-room and up to their rooms and collected their luggage and got into two cabs and departed.

I'm afraid the children didn't mind a bit. While this had been going on in the drawing-room, they had been busy changing over the contents of the suitcases: and all they could think of was big fat Nanny tomorrow, trying to struggle into the skinny little nursery-maid's dresses; and what the two starchy nurses would look like in Mademoiselle's Paris hats.

'Oh, dear,' sighed Mr and Mrs Brown, 'we shall have to get a new staff of governesses and nurses and nannies.' So they ordered the carriage and drove round to the Agency. The Agency was doubtful, because they had already sent rather a lot of nurses and nannies and governesses to Mr and Mrs Brown's family. 'The person *you* want,' they said, 'is Nurse Matilda.'

'I'm afraid we don't know any Nurse Matilda,' said Mr and Mrs Brown. So the Agency rather reluctantly agreed to send a new nursery staff to the Brown family.

So on Monday a cab drew up at the gate

and out of it poured a new fat nanny and a new governess and two new starchy nurses; and a skinny little nursery-maid, as usual, to wait on them all. Mr and Mrs Brown left the drawing-room and hurried to the front door, all welcoming smiles. But what was their amazement to see nothing but one skinny leg of the nursery-maid disappearing, as she was hauled into the cab – and five horror-stricken faces gazing backwards and upwards as the whole party drove off down the road as fast as it could go. Mr and Mrs Brown rushed out into the drive and looked up, themselves.

At every window of the house (except the drawing-room) stood a group of children, their hair on end, their faces twisted into horrible grimaces, their arms dreadfully waving as they mopped and mowed and lolloped about, obviously in the last stages of the worst kind of lunacy.

'My children!' gasped Mrs Brown. 'My poor, dear, darling children! The dogs have gone mad and bitten them and now they've all gone mad too!'

'Rabies!' cried Mr Brown.

'Hydrophobia!' cried Mrs Brown.

'Raving!' cried Mr Brown.

'Foaming at the mouth!' cried Mrs Brown.

'Only they aren't,' said Mr Brown, calming down a bit and looking up at the children, whose faces were certainly quite innocent of foam; and he looked at the dogs which had rushed out gaily into the garden to speed the departing cab, and added: 'And *they* aren't.' And he grew very thoughtful.

But Mrs Brown was already flying upstairs. She was very sweet, but she was really rather foolish about her poor, dear, darling children. Of course her poor, dear, darling children hadn't been bitten by mad dogs at all, and of course they weren't mad either.

So Mr and Mrs Brown ordered the carriage and drove round to the Agency again.

The Agency was quite cross. 'You simply must get Nurse Matilda,' they said.

'But we don't *know* any Nurse Matilda,' said Mr and Mrs Brown.

'Well – for the very last time,' said the Agency.

'Oh, thank you,' said Mr and Mrs Brown, and they drove hopefully home. At least Mrs Brown was hopeful. I'm not so sure about Mr Brown.

As it happened, Mr and Mrs Brown had

to go out on the following day, so they said to
the butler, who was a large, sad, dignified man
called Hoppitt, much given to having Feelings
in his Bones, 'Hoppitt, if the new nursery
staff arrive in the meantime, please give them
a nice welcome and take them upstairs to the
schoolroom to meet the children.'

'Yes, Sir, yes, Madam,' said Hoppitt, but he
thought to himself, Do you call *that* a nice
welcome? He had a Feeling in his Bones at
this very moment; and it was that Mr and
Mrs Brown had been foolish to tell their children how anxious they had been, about their
being bitten by mad dogs, and going mad too.

But Mr and Mrs Brown had never thought
of that and they drove off, quite untroubled,

and on their way back they said to one another, gladly, 'We're earlier than we hoped. Perhaps we'll be in time to meet the new staff, after all.'

Well, they were – in a way. The new staff had just burst out of the front door as Mr and Mrs Brown's carriage drew up to the gate and were streeling down the drive in terrified con-fusion, led by the governess – she was German, this time – bellowing, *'Hilfe! Hilfe! Die Hunde sind verruckt!'* with a fat nanny waddling frantically in her wake, gasping out, 'Oh, my poor 'eart!' and the two starchy nurses shoving along behind her, hooting, 'Out of our way! Out of our way!' The skinny little nursery-maid dodged between them all, like a boy on a bicycle nipping through the traffic, screeching in a dreadful monotony, 'Ow! Ow! Ow!'

And as they all hurled and tumbled towards the gate, there appeared behind them, to the horror of Mr and Mrs Brown, two small creatures, one brown, one black, their faces covered with a lather of shaving-soap, laced through with tomato ketchup – which ran, barking shrilly and nipping at the heels of the departing staff, while all the children danced in the background crying, 'Run for your lives! Don't let them bite you! They're mad . . . !'

So the next day, Mr and Mrs Brown ordered the carriage, and drove round to the Agency. They didn't wait for the Agency to say anything. They asked at once, 'Can you find Nurse Matilda for us?'

'No, we can't,' said the Agency shortly – for they had heard from the German governess and the nurses and the nanny and the skinny little nursery-maid, as they all streaked through the town on their way to the anti-hydrophobia clinic. And they added firmly: 'And we have Nobody Else On Our Books.'

'Oh, dear!' said Mr and Mrs Brown, and they got into their carriage and drove off to another Agency.

And to another Agency . . .

And to *another* Agency . . .

But it was no good. All the agencies had heard by now all about Mr and Mrs Brown's children and they just shut the door in their faces and peered out through the crack and advised them strongly to get Nurse Matilda.

'If only we could,' sighed poor Mr and Mrs Brown as, at the end of the long day, they took off their hats and coats in the hall.

And as they spoke – lo and behold! – there was a knock at the door, and there stood a small, stout figure dressed in rusty black; and she said, 'Good evening, Mr and Mrs Brown, I am Nurse Matilda.'

Well!

She was very ugly – the ugliest person you ever saw in your life! Her hair was scraped into a bun, sticking straight out at the back of her head like a teapot handle; and her face was very round and wrinkly, and she had eyes like two little black boot-buttons. And her nose! – she had a nose like two potatoes. She wore a rusty black dress right up to the top of her neck and right down to her button boots, and a rusty black jacket and a rusty black bonnet, all trimmed with trembly black jet, with her teapot-handle of a bun sticking out at the back. And she carried a small brown case and a large black stick, and she had a very fierce expression indeed on her wrinkly, round, brown face.

But what you noticed most of all was that she had one huge front Tooth, sticking right out like a tombstone over her lower lip. You never, in the whole of your life, ever saw such a Tooth!

Mrs Brown was quite aghast at the sight of the Tooth. Her poor, dear, darling, blameless angels! She faltered: 'I'm not sure that . . . Well, I mean . . . I don't really know that we need you after all,' and, politely but firmly, she started to close the door.

'Oh, yes, you do,' said Nurse Matilda, and she tapped at the door with her big black stick. Hoppitt usually opened the door – you would hear his dignified footsteps marching un hurriedly towards it – but this time, before he had even appeared from his pantry – suddenly Mr and Mrs Brown found that Nurse Matilda was in the hall with them, and the front door shut after them – if it had ever opened, and they couldn't remember that it had.

'I understand that your children are *exceedingly* naughty,' said Nurse Matilda.

Poor Mrs Brown! 'I don't think . . . I'm quite sure . . . Well, I mean, they're not exactly *naughty*—'

'Yes, they are,' said Mr Brown.

'Mischievous, perhaps. High spirited. Fun loving . . .'

'Naughty,' said Mr Brown.

So Mr and Mrs Brown began . . .

'It's true that they won't go to bed—'

'And won't get up—'

'And won't do their lessons—'

'And won't shut doors after them—'

'And won't wear their best clothes—'

'And they do gobble their food—'

'And they will keep running away,' admitted Mrs Brown.

'And they never say "Please" and "Thank you",' added Mr and Mrs Brown together. 'And of course—'

'That will do to go on with,' said Nurse Matilda. 'Your children need me.'

'Well, perhaps,' agreed Mrs Brown doubtfully. 'But,' she added, looking at the Tooth again, 'I don't want to hurt your feelings, but – suppose they don't *want* you ?'

'The more they don't want me,' said Nurse Matilda, 'the more they must need me. That is the way I work. When my children don't want me, but do need me: then I must stay. When they no longer need me, but they do want me: then I have to go.' And she smiled at Mr and Mrs Brown, and suddenly it seemed to them that, just for a moment, she wasn't really quite so ugly after all. There was even, Mrs Brown thought, a tear in her bright little boot-button eye. 'It's rather sad,' said Nurse Matilda; 'but there it is!' And she handed her little brown case to Mr Brown to put down by the umbrella-stand in the hall and, still holding her big black stick, started off up the stairs. 'Your children will require seven lessons,' said Nurse Matilda. 'To go to bed when they're told,' she said on the first step. 'Not to gobble,' she said on the second step. 'To do their lessons,' she said on the third step. 'To get up when they're called,' she said on the fourth step. 'To close doors after them, to wear their best clothes when they have to; and not to run away,' she said on the fifth, sixth and seventh steps. '"Please" – and – "Thank – you" – will – look – after – them – selves,' she added on the remaining nine steps up to the turn of the stairs, one word to a step; and she turned and looked down at Mr and Mrs Brown, standing helpless, gazing back at her from the hall. 'Don't trouble about me. I shall find my own way,' said Nurse Matilda and stumped on up to the first floor, where the schoolroom was.

Chapter 2

 HEN Nurse Matilda opened the schoolroom door, the children had finished their supper and were waiting for bedtime – though of course they had no intention of going to bed. And this is what they were doing:

Francesca had filled the Tiny Baby's bottle with baby-food and was feeding the dogs with it.

Little Quentin had drawn flowers all up the walls and was watering them from the big, brown, nursery teapot.

Antony was filling up the nursery ink-wells with runny red jam.

Nicolas had collected all the Little Ones' dolls and was lining them up for execution.

Sophie was shampooing Henrietta's hair with glue.

All the other children were doing simply dreadful things too.

When Nurse Matilda came in, they all went straight on with what they were doing.

'Good evening, children,' said Nurse Matilda, and she gave a loud thump on the floor with her big black stick. 'I am Nurse Matilda.'

Nobody took the faintest notice; but Christianna gave a large wink at the rest of them and said, 'How funny! The door's opened, but nobody has come in.'

They all knew quite well that the door had opened and Nurse Matilda had come in.

'And now it's closed again,' said Caro, 'and still nobody has come in.'

'*I* have come in,' said Nurse Matilda. 'I am Nurse Matilda.'

'Did anyone speak?' said Jaci, pretending to seem surprised.

'*I* didn't hear anything,' said Almond.

'*I* didn't hear anyfink,' said Little Sarah.

'Go gear, go gear!' cried the Baby, joyfully. This was the language the Baby spoke – all of its own.

'Well, all listen carefully,' said Nurse Matilda, 'and try to hear this. You are to stop what you're doing and put all your things away and go to bed.'

Everybody went straight on with what he was doing. Francesca went on feeding the dachshunds, Quentin went on watering the nursery walls, Antony went on pouring jam into the ink-wells . . .

Nurse Matilda looked them all over quietly with her black, beady eyes; and then she thumped once more on the floor with her stick.

After a while, the jam ran out over the top of the ink-well and all over Antony's hands. He licked it off, but he still went on pouring, the jam still went on running over, and he had to lick and lick and soon he felt quite sick. This is silly, he thought. All I've got to do is to stop pouring jam into the ink-well! But he couldn't stop: try as he would, he couldn't stop pouring jam into the ink-well and so the jam went on running and he went on licking, and soon he was feeling a very ill boy indeed. He cast a despairing look at Nicolas.

Nicolas had executed all the dolls – they lay in a long row, headless, and now he seemed to be casting round for more victims, teddy bears, golliwogs, stuffed animals of every kind. The Little Ones, stricken to their hearts by this massacre of their treasures, were howling

dismally, clinging to his legs and arms, pulling
his hair half out, in their anxiety – and yet he
went on collecting, went on lining the poor
creatures up and, whack, whack, whack,
lopping off their sad heads. Even his own
precious army of tin soldiers was now in a
neat row, stolidly waiting to die.

And Francesca was stuffing baby-food down
the dogs' throats, stuff, stuff, stodge, stodge,
and the dogs were full up with baby-food
right to the top, and they didn't like it any
more and were fearsomely growling. Francesca
looked scared – she had never known Sugar

and Spice to growl before; and *they* were looking surprised because they never did growl;
but still she went on feverishly mixing baby-
food and every time they opened their mouths
to give another growl, she poked more food
down them.

And Quentin went on pouring and pouring
tea down the walls and the teapot seemed quite
inexhaustible. The floor was two inches deep
in tea, and their feet were all wet; and everyone
who wasn't executing dolls or feeding dogs or
licking jam or shampooing hair – by this time
Sophie and Hetty were stuck together like
Siamese twins, struggling stickily to get apart,
but Sophie still went on pouring glue over
Hetty's head, both of them weeping with rage
and resentment – by this time, everyone who
wasn't otherwise employed, was stamping
about with soaking wet feet, quite brown with
tea water, telling Quentin to stop it. But
Quentin wouldn't stop it. The fact was that
he *couldn't* stop it. Any more than Francesca
or Antony or Nicolas or Sophie could stop
it . . .

And by now all they longed to do was to
stop it and go to bed. But you see, they
couldn't.

Well, they didn't like giving in. But at last they did say, crossly and grudgingly: 'Oh, do let's stop this and go to bed.'

'Say "Please",' said Nurse Matilda.

'We never say "Please",' said the children.

'Well, then, you'll never get to bed,' said Nurse Matilda.

'Oh, all right – "Please", then,' said the children.

'Peag, geng,' said the Baby, in its own language.

And Nurse Matilda looked at them and she smiled a little smile: and – it was very odd, but just for a moment her fierce round face with its boot-button eyes and its nose like two potatoes, didn't look quite so fierce after all: and except for the Tooth, not even quite so ugly.

And she gave one sharp rap with her stick on the floor – and all of a sudden, the floor began to dry up and all the tea began to run glop, glop, glop, *backwards*, into the teapot. And all the tins of baby-food were empty, which they hadn't been up to that minute, and the bottle stopped pouring itself into the dogs and they gave themselves a great shake, no growls any more, and ran off quite hungrily to have their own dinners from the bowls in the nursery corner. And Nicolas stopped executing dolls and their heads flew back again, ping, ping, ping, on to their necks. And Sophie and Hetty came apart with a terrific squelch and the glue ran in a little river towards the dolls and got between their heads and their necks and stuck their heads back on again . . .

And Nurse Matilda gave another sharp rap with her stick; and in that one second, it seemed to the children, every child was sitting in its nice, warm, cosy bed, all clean and neat, hands scrubbed, face washed, teeth brushed, hair combed, prayers said – with no idea in the world as to how it got there.

Nurse Matilda went quietly downstairs and reported to Mr and Mrs Brown. 'Lesson One,' she said.

Chapter 3

BEFORE breakfast next morning, Nurse Matilda sent the children out to the garden for some Healthful Fresh Air. When she called them in again, this is what they were doing:

David had cut all the gardener's best marrows and put them into the pigsty; and the old sow was at her wit's end, because she thought she had suddenly got eight brand-new babies to look after. Stephanie had made herself a nose out of two potatoes and was pretending to be Nurse Matilda. Toni had persuaded the Little Ones that they were really ducks and they were sitting in the muddy grass round the pond, earnestly trying to lay eggs.

And the Baby had toddled down to the front gate and was pleading, 'Alms for ge lovey Aggy!' and holding out the little nursery potty to passers by.

All the other children were doing simply dreadful things too.

Nurse Matilda appeared at the breakfast-room window and rang a large bell. No one took any notice. David added a ninth marrow to the family of the distracted old sow. Stephanie banged about with a large stick (but I must admit, she did it with her face turned away from the real Nurse Matilda); Toni urged on the Little-ies in their egg-laying efforts. And then, suddenly . . . A funny sort of feeling began to creep over the children . . . Supposing that, once again, it wasn't so much that they *wouldn't* stop, as that they *couldn't* stop!

They all stopped rather quickly, while they still could: and went in to breakfast.

After a little while Nurse Matilda said: 'There is no need to gobble.'

But they did gobble. They always gobbled. They liked breakfast. They liked their porridge so stiff that it would spin round in its own milk like a little island. They liked to write their names, each on his own island of porridge, with a thin thread of treacle dripping from the spoon. And they liked their boiled eggs, and turned them upside down in the egg-cups when they'd finished, to look like whole new eggs; and they liked their mugs of milk or tea, and their lovely fresh home-made bread and butter. So they went on gobbling: snatching bread and butter from under one another's noses, scooping out the last of the jam without caring who else wanted it, holding out their mugs for more, without a 'Please' or 'Thank you' . . .

Nurse Matilda sat at the top of the table, her big black stick in her hand.

Down went the porridge, down went the eggs, down went the bread and butter and jam.

And more bread and butter and jam.

And *more* bread and butter and jam.

And *more* bread and butter and jam and *more* bread and butter and jam and MORE and MORE and MORE bread and butter and jam . . .

'Here,' said the children with their mouths full, 'that's enough!' only their mouths were so full that what they said sounded like 'Assawuff,' and Nurse Matilda only looked politely puzzled and said, 'Did you ask for more porridge?' and to every child's utter horror, there before it was a plate of porridge all over again, spinning dizzily with its golden signature in its sea of milk. And their hands

seized up their spoons and down went the
porridge, stuff, stuff, stodge, stodge, on top of
all that bread and butter. And suddenly all
those upside-down eggshells really *were* full, new
eggs; and up and down flashed their egg-
spoons choking down egg on top of porridge;
and on top of the egg came more and more of
that dreadful bread and butter and jam . . .
And then the porridge started all over again . . .

The children puffed and blew, their cheeks
bulged, their eyes goggled. They felt that at

any moment they would blow up and burst. They longed to cry out for mercy. They would even have said 'Please' if they had thought of it. They would have done anything if only they could have stopped eating. But they couldn't; until at last they suddenly had a brilliant idea. The next time the porridge came round, they forced and fought with their own right hands until the hands just managed to write, with treacle, on the islands of porridge, 'STOP!'

Nurse Matilda looked at the plates of porridge. 'Say "Please",' she said.

They had to wait all through the eggs and the bread and butter till porridge came round again; and then write 'PLEASE!'

And Nurse Matilda smiled. (And really, was she quite so ugly as they had thought her last night?) And she banged with her big

black stick on the floor; and suddenly all the children were standing up quietly behind their chairs and saying their grace.

Nurse Matilda joined Mr and Mrs Brown, who were having their own breakfast in the dining-room. 'Lesson Two,' she said.

Chapter 4

WHEN Nurse Matilda went up to the schoolroom to begin the first morning's lessons, the children were sitting all round the huge table as good as gold. She sat down and looked round at them steadily. She said: 'Why are Sophie and Hetty wearing their hats?'

'They can't get used to having short hair,' said Simon. 'They're shy of showing their long ears.' And he added: 'It's very awkward, but they seem to have turned into dachshunds.'

'And we've turned into children,' said two very growly voices from under the table.

Nurse Matilda lifted a corner of the red, bobble-edged schoolroom tablecloth, and there, curled up on the floor, were the dachshunds; which, however, certainly did look very much like two little girls in brown Holland pinafores. And she looked beneath the brims of the round, grey felt hats, and saw two long, goldeny jowls, and two black, moist noses, and two pairs of bright, slightly bewildered eyes. And she gave a little tap with her stick and at once there came from under the table two short, sharp barks and she said: 'Oh, dear, I think the dogs need to be let out,' and bent down and took them by the scruffs of their pinafores and led them to the door and down the stairs and into the garden: and pushed them outside and closed the garden door on them. And try as they might to say, 'We're only pretending, we're not really dachsies at all, we're really Sophie and Hetty,' all they could do was to utter piteous growls and whines.

Nurse Matilda went back to the schoolroom. She said: 'We will begin with arithmetic.'

'Umps rumps,' said all the children, readily.

'What do you mean?' said Nurse Matilda.

'Oh, don't you know?' said Tora. 'That's Fuddledutch. We once had a Fuddledutch governess and I'm afraid we can't do arithmetic in anything else.' She repeated it in Fuddledutch (a language known only to the Brown children). 'We wumps humps a Fuddledumps gumpsmumps and we cumps dumps Arumpsmatumps in anythumps umps.'

'I see,' said Nurse Matilda: and she turned
a page and asked in perfect Fuddledutch (only
far faster than any of them could speak it):
'Well, then, humps mumps is thumpety
thrumps divumps bumps numps?'

Roger tried to say, 'Seventy-three divided
by nine goes eight and three over,' but he
couldn't. He found himself answering, 'Umps
and thrumps umps.'

'Wrong,' said Nurse Matilda and she turned

to the golden-brown faces beneath the round felt hats.

'Eight and one over,' said two rather barky voices in unison; and two pairs of bright, little, twinkly eyes looked out from beneath the hat brims with kindly pity.

'Right. But the rest of you had better all learn your tables. Now then: Twice one are two . . .' said Nurse Matilda. She added, sharply: 'Sit up!'

The children continued to lounge in their chairs, and they said not a word – not even, 'Twumps wumps are twumps.' But already they were doubtful. Already, deep within them, little voices were saying, 'Are you quite wise . . . ?' And, sure enough, even as they lounged there, the backs of the chairs – those dear old familiar schoolroom chairs, where they had lounged through their lessons with all their poor, harassed governesses up to now – seemed very hard and high; and the backs poked into *their* backs, and the seats had little splinters which stuck into *their* seats, if they wriggled; and if they tipped backwards only just the littlest bit, the whole chair went over with a crash and landed them on the floor with their legs in the air – and there they

stuck! By the time the morning break came, every one of them was sitting up straight except those who were lying on their backs, looking silly, with their legs in the air.

When the time came for cocoa and biscuits at eleven, Nurse Matilda took hers with Mr and Mrs Brown in Mrs Brown's little boudoir.

'How are the children progressing?' said Mr Brown.

'I think we have mastered Lesson Three,' said Nurse Matilda, smiling; and after she had gone back to the schoolroom, Mrs Brown said to Mr Brown, 'Do you know, when she smiles she really looks almost pretty. Except, of course,' she added, 'for that terrible Tooth.'

Chapter 5

NEXT morning the children wouldn't get up.

Some days it was like that – they just *wouldn't* get up. The nurses and governesses used to beg them and plead with them, and get them by the arms and tug at them, but they wouldn't get up. If at last some of them were bodily pulled out of bed, then they waited till the grown-ups turned their attention to some of the others, and by the time the poor exhausted nurses looked round, the first lot had hopped back into bed and humped the blankets over their heads and were making dreadful noises, pretending to snore. Once they all got into bed upside-down, and the nurses got awful shocks because when they angrily pulled back the bed-clothes and said, 'Get up!' there were two feet asleep on the pillow. And once they all swopped beds with each other, and Nanny nearly had a fit, because when she went to get the Baby from the cot it was making the most peculiar noises, and she thought *it* was having a fit, but it was really huge Simon curled up, nearly bulging the sides of the cot out, and the noise was him, trying to stop laughing. And once they all put dummies in their beds and got under the beds, and Nanny and the nurses and the governess all got more shocks; though perhaps that wasn't exactly not getting up. But, anyway, on this morning, they wouldn't.

Nurse Matilda stood in the doorway and now I'm afraid she didn't look pretty at all; and not a bit smiley, either – short and squat, she looked, like an angry old toad, in her rusty black dress, with her hair done up at the back in its teapot handle and her little dark eyes all glittery and her great big Tooth, and her nose like two potatoes; holding her big black stick. She said for the second time: 'Get up!'

Everybody snored dreadfully. Nobody moved.

Nurse Matilda lifted her big black stick and suddenly all the snores stopped. Eyes opened and peeped out from beneath the humps of blankets. They couldn't help remembering those other times when Nurse Matilda had banged with her stick.

Nurse Matilda noted the silence and the bright eyes peeping and she lowered her stick. 'I shall give you half an hour,' she said, 'to be up and dressed and washed, teeth cleaned, pyjamas folded, windows opened, beds turned back; and out into the garden for some Healthful Fresh Air before breakfast. The Big Ones will look after the Little Ones.' And she went away.

Well!

They were out of bed in two seconds after her back was turned – but not to wash and dress. They had never given way before and they weren't going to now. On the other hand – that stick! There was a great scuttering between the boys' rooms and the girls' rooms, to confer; a great deal of whispering and planning; a great flurry of activity – a wild scampering back to bed when Nurse Matilda's footfall was heard once more. When Nurse Matilda said, 'Why haven't you got up?' they all said: 'We can't get up. We're ill.'

'Ill?' said Nurse Matilda. (And it *was* very sudden.)

'We've got codes id our dozes,' said Roger.

'Ad paids id our piddies,' said Tora.

'Ad spots,' said Louisa.

'Ad tebratures,' said Simon.

'Ad we feel sick,' said Fenella.

'We thig id bust be the beasles,' said Teresa.

'All gock meagig,' said the Baby in its own language.

And, sure enough, when Nurse Matilda looked, she saw that their faces were as white as clowns', and covered with huge red (paint-box) spots.

'Very well,' said Nurse Matilda; and she banged once with her stick and went away. The children started immediately to scramble out of bed. But . . . Yes – you've guessed! They couldn't. They just had to stay there, humped under the blankets – which were suddenly dreadfully hot and scratchy – and their noses felt dreadfully stuffy and they had pains in their pinnies and weren't at all sure

that they weren't really going to be sick. And they put up their languid hands to their hot faces and tried to wipe away the spots – and the spots wouldn't go. And the dreadful truth dawned upon them at last: *they really had got measles.*

Poor Mrs Brown was in a terrible state when she learned that all her children had got measles.

'Leave it to me,' said Nurse Matilda calmly. 'I quite understand the disease.' And she laid down her rules. No noise. No light. Nothing to eat or drink. And of course – *no getting out of bed.*

Mrs Brown was horrified. Her poor, darling children! 'Nothing to eat?'

'Not while they have these pains.'

'And nothing to drink?'

'Not while they feel so sick.'

'No noise? Not even talking—?'

'Not while their colds are so bad that they talk through their noses.'

'And no light? Can't they even look at books?'

'Not while they have such high temperatures!' said Nurse Matilda, quite shocked. She added: 'However, of course there will be

Doses.' And she produced three huge bottles of medicine and ranged them side by side on the mantelpiece: a black bottle and a red bottle and a dreadful yellowy-green bottle.

'For the fever,' said Nurse Matilda, going round with the black bottle.

'For the pains,' she said, going round with the red bottle.

'For the spots,' she said, going round with the yellowy-green bottle.

The yellowy-green one was the worst; but, all in all they were three of the nastiest medicines the Brown children had ever had to take in all their lives. They had a large tablespoon of each of them, every single hour.

'*Hog*gig meggikig,' said the Baby.

'No talking,' said Nurse Matilda – even to the Baby.

It was a long, long day. To Mr and Mrs Brown, it seemed like ten days, which is the time that measles usually lasts; and I can assure you it seemed like ten days to the children too. There they lay, huddled up under the hot, prickly blankets, and their heads ached and their tummies ached and they felt sick, and when they raised their poor, dull heads to look at the others, the others looked awful, all covered with enormous spots. And of course as the hours passed by and the pains got better and they didn't feel so sick, they began to get dreadfully hungry. And only then did they remember that it was Wednesday and that Wednesday was their favourite dinner day. On Wednesday there was steak and kidney pudding, the crust dry and light on top and all sloshy and gooey underneath as it ought to be, wallowing in its hot, rich gravy; and mashed potatoes with a little cheese in them to make them all goldeny, and swedes, not boiled in water at all, but sliced up thin and cooked in nothing but butter (speciality of Cook). And treacle roly-poly, just as they loved it – not a solid bolster of pudding with some syrup poured over it, but a thin layer rolled out and spread with great dollops of treacle and then rolled up again lightly; so that every inch of it was simply oozy with gold . . .

I know it was a dreadfully indigestible meal, but Mrs Brown always gave her children whatever they liked best, every single day of the week.

But there was no steak and kidney, or treacle roll today. Instead, beneath their win-

dows they heard the tramp of feet and clatter of dishes and the voices of Hoppitt and Cook upon a melancholy mission. Hoppitt had placed a large table outside the gate, with a notice saying, SPARE STEAK-AND-KIDNEY PUDS, MASHED POTATOES, SWEDES (SPECIALITY OF COOK) AND TREACLE ROLY-POLIES FOR ANYONE WHO WANTS THEM. GOING WASTE ON ACCOUNT OF MEASLES. NO CHARGE, BUT PLEASE PUT ANYTHING YOU WISH TO DONATE INTO MONEY-BOX SUPPLIED.

I'm afraid the money-box supplied had been supplied by Hoppitt and Cook; but still it had been their idea in the first place.

So there the children lay and longed for steak-and-kidney pudding and treacle roly-poly and thought with rage and gloom that

45

the village children would be having the time of their lives. They waged continual war with the village children, who were led by a huge and terrible boy called Podge. He will be podgier than ever after this, thought the Brown children, resentfully.

But they must lie and suffer; and now that their headaches were going, they'd have liked to look at books, but the curtains were drawn and even if they could have seen to read, they weren't allowed to; and as for talking, every time they opened their mouths, Nurse Matilda was there with a large spoonful of medicine. By the time dusk fell and she came to tuck them up – she had to begin early, there were so many of them – and give them their final doses (double this time, 'To last them through the night'), the children were ready to say humbly, 'Tomorrow morning – can we get up?'

'Can you what?' said Nurse Matilda.

'Can we get up?'

'Can you what?' said Nurse Matilda.

'Cay peag,' said the Baby.

'Oh, yes: can we get up, *please*?' said the children.

And Nurse Matilda smiled and she gave a

little tap with her stick and she went away; and when she had gone the children never even mentioned the Tooth. They just said to one another, 'Just for a moment – didn't she look *pretty*?'

Next morning, when Nurse Matilda came to the door, the children were up and washed and dressed and had cleaned their teeth and folded their pyjamas and opened the windows and turned back their beds and were ready to go down to the garden for some Healthful Fresh Air before breakfast. The Big Ones were leading the Little Ones by the hand. Nurse Matilda said nothing; but she asked Hoppitt to take a message to Mr and Mrs Brown with their breakfast.

'Nurse's compliments, Madam,' said Hoppitt, 'and I am to say "Lesson Four".'

'Oh, thank you, Hoppitt,' said Mrs Brown. 'And do you know if the children are better?'

'That I don't know, Madam,' said Hoppitt. 'But I have – if you will pardon the expression, Sir and Madam – a Feeling in my Bones that they are going to be.' And he added, in a very rare burst of confidence: 'Nurse Matilda herself is *looking* – well, better, this morning.'

Chapter 6

 Y O U needn't think that from then on the Brown children were always good – indeed they weren't! They were naughty the very next day, as you're going to see. I suppose they were so much in the habit of it, that they couldn't get used to being good; and, anyway, they had only come to Lesson Four.

But just for that day, they *were* good; and they had to confess, even when they got naughty again, that they had had a wonderful time.

It was a lovely day and Nurse Matilda gave them their lessons in the garden. But such lessons! First they had history, and the lawn was the Atlantic Ocean, and the shrubbery on the other side of it was America, and they got out the old pony trap – fetched from the coachhouse – and that was the *Mayflower*; and they all piled in and sailed across the Atlantic, being frightfully seasick over the sides of the pony trap and constantly crying out, 'Land ahoy!' and being dreadfully disappointed when it wasn't. By the mid-morning break for milk and biscuits, even the Baby could say 'Game-ge-gurk,' and 'Kickgeen-hungigan-kenki', and 'Ge Gaykower,' which as Nurse Matilda seemed to know, quite without the children translating for her, meant James the First and sixteen hundred and twenty and the *Mayflower*. As *you* know, of course, that was when the *Mayflower* sailed.

And after the break they had French, and half the children were verbs and the other half were verb-endings, and they played a new kind of hide-and-seek, finding their own endings; and then it was time for lunch.

'This afternoon,' said Nurse Matilda when lunch was over, 'we will go for a walk – and do arithmetic.'

'Oh, lor'!' said the children, losing heart. (Fancy a *walk*! And *arithmetic*!)

But Nurse Matilda's arithmetic was very different from the governesses' arithmetic. Nurse Matilda made them pretend that they had only so many arms and legs between them,

49

not enough to go round. Some of them had to hop and some of them, who had no legs at all, had to be carried (fortunately these were mostly the smaller ones), and the armless ones had to walk along looking very stiff and stout with their coats buttoned right over their real arms, which were pinned down to their bodies by the buttoned-up coats, and their sleeves hanging empty. So then they began to re-divide the arms and legs, to try and even things out; and in this way the Little Ones learnt adding and taking away – 'take away one leg from Justin, who has two, and give it to poor Dominic, who has none. Arabella and Joanna and Susannah have four arms between them; give them one each, and that'll be three and one over . . .' And the Bigger Ones learnt money sums by making prices for an arm or a leg; and those who had too few, bargained with those who had enough – or, as soon happened if you were good at bargaining, too many.

Tora, who was terribly bad at arithmetic, ended up just a sort of pillow, poor thing, with – officially – no arms and legs at all; while Antony, who was always very good at money – perhaps because when he was little he had swallowed a penny and become rather a hero with his brothers and sisters – had four arms and three legs and somehow managed to be one and tuppence richer as well. However, he was a very kind boy and he went back and sold Tora a leg for her last tuppence, so at least she was able to hop; and he held her up, because, of course, having no arms, she couldn't hang on to him. Otherwise, as she was one of the Big Ones – too big to be carried – she'd have had to stay planted by the wayside, till they picked her up on the way back and lent her a leg, just to get home with.

That night, when Nurse Matilda saw them all into bed, she really did – except for the Tooth – look all smiles and almost beautiful. The children thought they would never, never, never be naughty again.

But next morning when they woke up, you won't be surprised to hear they were just as naughty as ever.

When Nurse Matilda sent them to get some Healthful Fresh Air before breakfast, they didn't go out at all. They said to one another, 'Let's go through the Baize Door.'

In those days, when there were such big families, they needed lots of people to look after them, and the houses were divided into two parts: very often by a door covered with baize – green or red – and studded with big, round brass nails. On one side of the Baize Door lived the Family, and on the other side lived the Staff. In the Browns' case, the Staff was Hoppitt and Cook; and Celeste, the French lady's maid, who looked after Mrs Brown; and Ellen, the parlourmaid, and Alice and Emily, the housemaids, who were always thought of like that, linked together like Siamese twins; and Evangeline, the 'tweeny'. Poor Evangeline, she was dreadfully put upon by the rest; but she was a cheerful little lump and I don't think she really minded.

Children – especially the Browns – were strictly forbidden ever to go through the Baize Door unless they were specially invited by the Staff. I must confess that the Brown children were very seldom invited.

But that morning – worn out by goodness, I suppose; they certainly weren't used to it – the children did go through the Baize Door; and what's more they didn't close it. You remember that one of the things Mr and Mrs Brown had told Nurse Matilda was that the children never could be got to close doors after themselves. 'Remember the Door!' their parents would cry out frantically. But the children never did. And they didn't close the Baize Door this morning, either.

Hoppitt and Cook and Celeste and Ellen and Alice and Emily were all having breakfast in the Staff Room (waited on by Evangeline) before the family breakfast was served. When they came back to the kitchen, this is what the children were doing:

Sophie had taken Hoppitt's grey woollen socks from the airer and was stirring them into the porridge.

Hetty had made a stiff paste of flour and water and was putting it through the mangle.

Justin had covered the seat of Cook's chair with dripping.

Almond had found Celeste's powder and paint and was giving the raw breakfast sausages dear little faces.

Agatha was giving the dogs a bath in the stock-pot.

And all the other children were doing simply dreadful things too.

The children took one look at Hoppitt and Cook and Celeste and Ellen and Alice and Emily, and ran out through the Baize Door as fast as they could, and shut it tight after them, and leant against it. On the other side, they could hear a fearful roaring and clucking and ooh-la-la-ing as Hoppitt and Cook and Celeste and Ellen and Alice and Emily found out what had happened to the socks and the mangle and the chair and the sausages and the stock-pot.

I'm afraid there was also a loud tee-hee-hee-ing; which, however, stopped abruptly as a commanding voice cried: 'Evangeline! – Get that door open!'

The children held on to the door with all their might. 'She can't!' they called back. 'We're safe!'

Nurse Matilda stood on the stairs above them, looking down; and she lifted her big black stick . . .

And the door swung suddenly inwards and all the children tumbled into the kitchen on top of one another, in a heap of arms and legs and heads and shoulders, and conveniently up-turned behinds.

Hoppitt and Cook, without a word, handed to Evangeline a large, flat frying-pan.

Whack, whack, whack, went the frying-pan.

The children howled and struggled and

fought, and at last were all on their feet again
and back on the other side of the door. But
hold that door as they might – it wouldn't close.
It was very strange: all those children! – and
they couldn't get a door to close.

And as it swung to and fro, they could see
into the kitchen where Cook and Hoppitt and
Celeste and Ellen and Alice and Emily were
arming Evangeline for total war. She ad-
vanced at last, urged forward by willing arms
and conjurations to Be Brave! On her head
was a huge black enamel saucepan, down her
stout front hung a big roasting dish, in one
hand she carried the frying-pan (somewhat

dented now) and in the other, Cook's rolling-pin. On her large, round face was a look of great unwillingness and doubt; but behind her was Hoppitt with the carving fork, prodding her on.

The children began to back away through the hall to the front door. Cries of 'Open the door!' 'Make for the garden!' rent the air. 'Go in ge gargy! Oping ge gor!' cried the Baby, backing away as fast as its short, fat legs would carry it. As usual, its nappy seemed just about to fall down.

But, just as the other door wouldn't shut – the front door wouldn't open. They pulled and they tugged, they struggled with the lock, they rattled the big bolts, they swung on the chain, but nothing would open the door. And advancing upon them, armoured in tin, Evangeline approached with uplifted frying-pan. But . . .

'After all,' said Daniel, suddenly. 'It's only Evangeline.'

All the children stopped struggling with the door and stared. The door immediately flew open, but they took no notice of it.

'After all,' they said. 'It's only Evangeline.'

'Ongy Egangykeeng,' said the Baby.

Nurse Matilda looked down from the stairs. She looked at the faces of the children, all smiles of relief, and she looked at Evangeline's large, round, unwilling face; and she thumped once more with her stick. And in that very instant, out of the kitchen, helmeted in sauce-pans, hung about with baking-tins, armed with frying-pans and rolling-pins and brooms and mops and flat-irons and a huge pair of curling tongs (Celeste!) dashed Hoppitt and Cook and Celeste and Ellen and Alice and Emily; and brushed Evangeline aside and came on . . .

The children were out of that open door before it had time to close on them again, and into the garden.

The kitchen army gave chase. Down the drive . . . Across the wide lawn . . . Out of the shrubbery, into the high-walled kitchen garden; scrambling through netting, between tall bean-rows, dodging among raspberry canes . . . The Little Ones got lost in a forest of blackcurrant bushes, the Middling Ones tripped over marrow trailers and had to be gone back for and hoicked up and set running again; squashed tomato, overripe gooseberry exploded and skidded beneath their pounding feet. The Baby's nappy had come down and was right round its ankles.

Into the greenhouse – door wouldn't shut after them to keep the pursuers back; out through a window to a crash of breaking glass and the rage of the gardener . . . Over the wall, down the gravelled paths, leaping flowerbeds, tearing through rose-bushes, running, running, running . . .

Running so fast that before they even thought of the pond, they were teetering on the grassy bank – skidding – tippling – and at last, splish splosh! splish splosh! were headlong into the middle of it, up to their waists in water and mud.

Hoppitt and Cook and Celeste and Ellen

and Alice and Emily and Evangeline got to the bank and, with frantically flailing arms to keep their balance, came to a halt and stood glaring. The children moved into the middle of the pond and defiantly glared back.

Hoppitt, of course, had established himself as generalissimo. He made a commanding gesture. 'Come out!' he cried, and added an expression that Evangeline knew only too well. 'And do it smartish!'

'No,' said Lindy; and threw a lump of pond mud at him.

Well!

The mud took Hoppitt, bonk! on the middle of his nose. But his dignity never wavered.

'Very well,' he said. 'You've asked for it.'

And now the children saw that, through thick and thin, he had carried with him the porridge saucepan.

The pond was very large and shallow and also very muddy. The children, clustering together in the very centre of it, stood their ground – if you could call it ground when it was actually such very soft, gooey, oozy, chocolatey, brown-black mud. Cook and Celeste and Ellen and Alice-and-Emily and Evangeline fanned out and made a circle round the edge of it. There was no escape; and now Hoppitt was seen to be passing among his troops, handing out porridge-soaked socks.

The battle was on.

Fortunately, only Hoppitt was a very good aim. The children recovered the floating socks and returned them, with a little good, black mud added for interest. *Their* aim was much better and soon the faces round the pond were a curious lumpy grey, streaked with black: only the eyes stared out balefully from beneath the kitchen saucepans. The socks flew back and forth, but by now they were losing their splendid coatings of porridge. Hoppitt dipped them back into the saucepan and reissued them. The children used the interval to wash their own faces in the pond. The effect was somewhat stripy, and bindweed tangled itself over them and hung down about their ears, like green hair; but at least they didn't have to keep licking in porridge. The staff on the bank couldn't wash, and beneath the cold oatmeal, their poor faces were growing very stiff.

When the porridge was exhausted, Cook produced the dough from the mangle.

The children were beginning to get rather desperate. All they had to fight back with was mud; and now Alice and Emily had armed themselves with mops and brooms, and every time a child stooped to scoop up more mud, it found itself held under with a large kitchen mop. Fortunately, the Littlest Ones, who might have been a difficulty, were simply loving it. With all those nannies and nurses and governesses, they had very seldom had a chance to play in really dirty water. (I think Nurse Matilda, when she banged with her stick, always saw that the Little Ones didn't suffer too badly.)

But even to entertain the Little Ones, you couldn't stand throwing mud and dough for ever: especially as, now that the dough was finished, Hoppitt could simply send Evangeline to the kitchen for fresh ammunition.

'Bring them sausages that they drew faces on,' he commanded.

'And all them jellies and blancmanges,' added Cook, 'that I set aside for nursery tea.'

The children took counsel among themselves.

'What we want is a hostage!'

'A gockig, a gockig!' cried the Baby, splashing up and down in the mud, looking like a chocolate baby, made to be eaten.

'I'll get Cook,' said Sally, at once.

Cook was laughing. She was standing at the edge of the pond with Hoppitt, and she was laughing at the thought of the children seeing all their lovely jellies and blancmanges used as ammunition. But the children really hated jelly and blancmange and had only ever pretended to eat them, so as not to hurt Cook's feelings. It did seem ungrateful of her to be laughing – and, anyway, so unlike Cook to be unkind. But everything was – well, *strange* – today.

Cook was laughing so much that she never even noticed Sally, slithering up out of the mud like an otter, and tying her stout ankles together with a piece of bindweed. When Evangeline returned, tacking across the lawn towards them, quite blinded by her high load of jellies and blancmanges, with the sausages coiled on top, Cook reached out and took the sausages, and threw one end straight at the huddle of children in the pond: and kicked her legs up in the air with joy.

But instead of her legs going two ways, as she intended – being tied together, they both went the same way; and Cook sat down upon her broad sit-upon, with a bump that shook the banks of the pond and set the jellies and blancmanges all a-wobble; and, well greased with the dripping that the children had put on her chair – she began to slide down the grassy slope towards the water. And the children seized one end of the chain of sausages and

tugged: and in her bewilderment, Cook quite forgot to let go of the other end.

It was a pretty desperate situation, all round. On the bank, Hoppitt and Ellen had got hold of Cook by the ears – her hair was not her own, so there was no use hanging on to that – and were holding on for dear life, to prevent her being taken hostage. In the pond, the children hauled on the line of sausages and drew her slowly down.

But the bottom of the pond was soft and slithery, and gradually their weight, as they hauled, was driving them deeper and deeper down into it – down to their ankles, down to their knees – the Little Ones were in it up to their waists . . . Yet they dared not let go or they would lose their hostage; and then here they would be, stuck fast in the mud, a helpless prey to onslaughts of jelly and blancmange; not to mention the brooms and mops and even the rolling-pin and the flat-iron and Celeste's curling tongs. What nips Celeste would give them with those curling tongs when she remembered her lost powder and paint, all lavished on those little smiling sausage faces . . . !

And meanwhile the mud was almost up to their necks. Oh dear, thought the children, if

only we hadn't gone through the Baize Door!
If only we could have got it to shut! For that
matter, they couldn't help ruefully adding, if
only we *ever* shut doors!

And as they said it, the Baby cried gleefully
(large bubbles of mud coming out of its
mouth, it being so much shorter than the
others and nearly submerged by now),
'Gairg Nurk Magiggy!'

And there she was indeed: standing quietly
on the lawn, watching them – though they
felt quite sure she hadn't been there before.

'Oh, Nurse Matilda,' they all cried out, 'do
help us!'

'Cay peag,' said the Baby; but almost before it had said it – this time, they all added:
'Please!'

And Nurse Matilda smiled; and as she
smiled, suddenly all sorts of things began to
happen. As Hoppitt and Ellen hauled, and
the children hauled, with the line of smiling
sausages stretched out taut between them, a
small *brown* shape flew through the water and
a set of sharp little white teeth bit through the
chain of sausages. And at the same time, a
little *black* shape flew up the bank and, with
another set of white teeth, snapped up Cook's

hair from between Hoppitt's and Ellen's hands and fled off across the lawn with it. And Hoppitt and Ellen were so astonished to find Cook with a bald pink head on top of her round, mud-black face, that they let go of her ears and she slid right down off the bank and into the arms of the enemy. At the same time, with great suckings and squelchings, the children's feet came suddenly out of the mud.

They were free! They had their hostage, the enemy was staring, helpless, from the bank. All they needed was some ammunition of their own, and the day was theirs.

'Oh, Nurse Matilda,' they prayed in their hearts. 'Please! *Please!*'

And Nurse Matilda smiled again; and Evangeline, whose pile of jellies and blanc-manges was still too high for the poor thing to see where she was going – eager all this time to find out what on earth was happening all about her – walked slap into the pond, tripped over some bindweed, tipped slowly forward and deposited her load bang in front of the children . . .

Hoppitt and Celeste and Ellen and Alice and Emily took one look at poor Cook, quite bald and covered with chocolate-coloured mud; and at Evangeline standing with her empty tray, up to her stout middle in water – and turned tail and walked with dignity – back to the kitchen. Nurse Matilda came to the edge of the pond and held out her hand, to help Cook ashore.

Cook was furious.

'Well! Just wait till Madam hears about *this*!' She stood, knee high in water, and you could see a week's notice written all over her face – in letters of mud. 'Let – me – tell – you, Nurse—' began Cook.

Nurse Matilda stood with her left hand held out; and with her right hand she raised her big black stick and gave a little thump. And almost before the thump had hit the ground, Cook's face had changed. 'Let me tell you, Nurse,' repeated Cook, taking the outstretched hand and hauling herself cheerfully up, 'that without those dear children, I don't know *where* I'd've been! Whatever come over me, I cannot imagine! Me toupee must have blown off – it often slips a bit: the Staff's quite used to it – and in running for it, I must have fell into the water. I'm not so nippy on me pins as I used to be,' admitted Cook, laughing good-naturedly. 'And those poor children must've all dived in and got theirselves wet, trying to help me out. Well, that *was* thoughtful of them! And I declare!' cried Cook, 'there's them good, kind dogs fetching me hair back to me!' Sure enough, Sugar had joined Spice and, having golloped up the sausages (little faces and all), they were now trotting quietly back, with Cook's hair carried delicately between them.

'So all's well that ends well,' said Nurse Matilda; and when the children had trooped into the house for hot baths and changes of clothes – closing every door carefully behind them, you can be quite certain – she went downstairs again and met Mrs Brown in the hall.

'Lesson Five,' said Nurse Matilda.

Chapter 7

THE children were very good all the next day, and even the Staff seemed softened by their experiences. Cook went to Mrs Brown and said that as Nurse thought the children should have a More Balanced Diet, however much she loved cooking roly-poly, and roast goose, with its thin, thin golden crackling, and swedes-in-butter (Speciality) and jellies and blancmanges – she would give it all up, and make boiled fish and rice-pudding so deliciously, that even they would like that just as much.

'I doubt if you – or even Nurse – will ever make them like greens,' said Mrs Brown.

'Well, perhaps not *greens*,' agreed Cook.

'I am sure they will just eat what they are given,' said Nurse Matilda, placidly; 'greens and all.'

And so they did. I can't say they liked the greens, but all the rest was so nice that in the end they didn't mind a Balanced Diet a bit, and even began to be quite glad not to have to feel rather ill after every meal. And, of course, they were privately *very* glad about the jellies and blancmanges.

So the days went happily by and one day Nurse Matilda said, 'Well, children, it is my Day Off. Be very good and do exactly what you are told. And don't forget – *greens* for lunch!' and she put on her rusty black jacket and her rusty black bonnet with its trembles of jet, and took her big black stick, and stumped off down the drive.

So the children settled down to play, and after a while Mrs Brown came to the school-room and said, 'Children, where is Nurse Matilda?'

This is what the children were doing when Mrs Brown came to the schoolroom:

Helen had stirred mud into the mid-morning cocoa and they'd all taken huge big first gulps.

Nicolas had his hands drawn up into his sleeves and was prowling about being the Armless Wonder and frightening the Little Ones.

Lindy had redressed Little Justin with both legs

70

in one trouser-leg and the poor boy was having to hop about like a robin.

Susannah had parachuted out of the window with an umbrella and landed in a manure heap: and now she was back again.

All the other children were being perfectly dreadful too.

Mrs Brown took one look at her dear children, armless, one-legged, choking up mud-and-cocoa and smelling of dung, and said, 'What a lovely time you seem to be having, darlings, but where is Nurse Matilda?'

So the children said, 'It's her day off. She's out.'

'Oh, dear,' said Mrs Brown. 'Well, darlings, your Great-Aunt Adelaide Stitch is coming to tea and she will wish to see you. So after lunch you must put on your best clothes.'

In the old days the children would have said to fat Nanny and the two starchy nurses and the governess – and even to their dear Mama, I'm afraid – 'Well, we jolly well won't.' But now they only grumbled and frowned and kicked the floor with the toes of their shoes (which is ruination to them) and growled out, 'Oh, *no? Need* we? We simply *hate* best clothes.'

71

'Poor darlings,' said Mrs Brown, 'but I'm afraid you must. Aunt Adelaide Stitch is very rich and she's going to leave all her money to your papa and me, because she's so sorry for us, having such a lot of you. So it's only fair to be nice to her.' And she added, 'And don't kick the floor with the toes of your shoes, it's ruination to them,' and went away quite happy and confident in the good behaviour of her darling children.

The children had a splendid time after Mrs Brown had left them. They went down to the gate and lay in wait for the lad Podge, as he came out of school. You've heard of Podge before. Besides being the leader of the village gang, he was the only son of his mother and father, Mr and Mrs Green. Mr and Mrs Green kept the sweet shop in the village, so I suppose that's why Podge was so immensely fat. He was dreadfully greedy.

There were so many of the children, and Podge, being alone – he was always first out of school when the break-for-dinner bell rang – it was easy for them to capture him. They tied him up into a sort of bundle and hid him behind the hedge. By the time the other village children arrived, the Browns were all

lolling about rubbing their stomachs and crying out, 'Ow! Ow! Ow!'

'What's the matter?' said the village children, delighted to see the suffering Browns.

'We were warned never to eat Boy,' said the Browns, 'and now we have and the grownups were quite right: he's given us awful pains.'

'What Boy?' asked the village children.

'Podge Green,' said the Browns. 'We chose him because there was the most meat on him.' And they began to straighten up and lick their chops a bit and look rather significantly round at the other village children, as though singling out the next fattest.

73

The children took to their heels and ran, and soon Podge's father and mother came streaking down the street crying, 'What have you done with him? What have you done with our boy?'

'Gone!' said the children – which was quite true, because they had meanwhile released Podge, who had made off across the fields as fast as his stout legs would carry him. But they rubbed their stomachs in a meaningful sort of way and shook their heads mournfully as though they wished he *hadn't* gone – as though they wished they could have begun on him all over again, so delicious had he been.

'Gone?' cried Mr and Mrs Green, looking wildly about them.

'All gone,' said the children, regretfully.

'Or gog!' echoed the Baby, rubbing its tummy too.

'What – even that innocent child—?' exclaimed Mr Green, staring in horror at the infant cannibal.

'It should still be on sieved vegetables,' cried Mrs Green, horrified too.

'And a little meat essence,' said Mr Green.

But the thought of meat essence and of their

poor boy boiled down to make it, was too much for the Podge parents. 'Help! Murder! Cannibalism!' they cried and, clutching at one another for support, they tottered off towards the police-station.

By the time Figgs, the village constable, had fully woken from his dinner-time nap (interrupted by the disturbing visit of Mr and Mrs Green), had run through his Police Manual for Instructions re Boy-eating in Rural Districts, and had buttoned up his uniform and found his helmet, Podge was back at his parents' home and was tucking into his middle-day dinner. (The meat, however, was pushed to one side of his plate.) Figgs saw the three of them as he passed on his way to the Browns', but he made no alteration in his purposeful progress. The boy Green had been reported Missing Believed Consumed by Cannibals; and Constable Figgs was going to investigate.

Hoppitt answered the door.

'I have come to Investigate,' said Constable Figgs.

'Investigate what?' said Hoppitt, smiling his superior, butler smile.

'Young Green,' said Figgs. 'Missing. Believed eaten.'

75

'Eaten?' cried Hoppitt, and his face quite lost its smile.

'Consumed on the premises, I understand,' said the constable, looking about him with interest.

'Follow me,' said Hoppitt, leading the way across the hall to the drawing-room. His mien was majestic still, but he was dreadfully pale. 'The C.I.D.,' he announced, flinging open the door and ushering the constable in; and he rushed off through the Baize Door to tell the rest of the Staff.

'Impossible!' cried Celeste. She said it in French, but it's the same word, anyhow.

'I wouldn't put it past them,' said Ellen, thinking it over.

'Had 'im for their dinner!' whispered Alice and Emily, aghast.

'After all them Balanced Meals!' said Cook.

Evangeline said nothing; but she glanced in the mirror at her own plump form and resolved to go on a diet from that moment on.

In the drawing-room, Constable Figgs had explained matters and Mr Brown had gone up to the nursery to summon the children. ('But I'm sure,' said Mrs Brown, 'that they can't have done anything so naughty.') They

filed in and stood in a ring on the drawing-room carpet.

'It 'as bin reported to me,' said Constable Figgs, looking down at them reproachfully, 'that you've ate up that young Green; had 'im for your dinner?'

'No, we haven't,' said the children. 'He was much too tough. Not Balanced enough, probably.' And they added, looking innocent, that they had only been doing exactly what they were told.

'What you were told?' cried Mrs Brown. 'Who ever told you to eat Podge Green?'

'Nurse Matilda,' said the children, respectfully.

'Gurk Magiggy,' said the Baby.

'Nurse Matilda! Told you to eat young Green—?' cried Constable Figgs.

'That's what she said,' said the children.

'Gack woggy keg,' said the Baby.

'But *what* did she say?' asked Constable Figgs and Mr and Mrs Brown, speaking all together.

'She said, "Green's for lunch",' said the children and the Baby, speaking all together too: only of course the Baby said, 'Geeng for gunk.'

'Green's for lunch!' said Constable Figgs: and he stood for a long time, quite still and quite silent, looking down at the toes of his big black boots. Then he took out his little black notebook and licked the lead of his big black pencil and wrote down: *Investigation into Outbreak of Cannibalism in Rural District*, and wrote after it in large black letters: CASE CLOSED; and closed the notebook too, and went away.

'There, you see!' said Mrs Brown, smiling happily at Mr Brown. 'I knew the children hadn't done anything so naughty.'

Chapter 8

ALL children have aunts and most children have at least one really fearsome aunt or even great-aunt. The Brown children had this truly fearsome great-aunt, Great-Aunt Adelaide Stitch.

Great-Aunt Adelaide Stitch was a terrible old person – very gaunt and tall, with an angry little eye like the eye of a rhinoceros. She had a nose a bit like a rhinoceros's too – like its horn, I mean, only of course it hooked downwards, not upwards like a horn. She knew the Catechism absolutely by heart, and she used to make the children stand in front of her – in their best clothes, of course – and recite it. Only, fortunately, there were so many of them that they never got beyond *What is your name?* because by the time they had got down to Arabella, Clarissa, Sarah, Joanna,

Timothy, Daniel, The Baby, the Tiny Baby, Sugar and Spice, she was worn out with the whole lot of them and didn't even go on to ask them *Who gave you your names?*

For some reason, Mr Brown was a little anxious about the afternoon ahead of them. 'I do hope the children will behave,' he said.

'Of course they will,' said Mrs Brown.

'What makes you think so ?' said Mr Brown, rather gloomily for him. He was usually very cheerful, but he did sometimes worry in case Aunt Adelaide Stitch should go back on her promise to leave them all her money; because with such a lot of children, and so many people to look after them all, and such a big house to keep them all in, it did cost a dreadful lot. 'I wouldn't want the children to offend her,' he said, 'when – underneath – she's really so kind.'

'Oh, I'm sure they won't offend her,' said Mrs Brown.

'Well, what about last time ?' said Mr Brown. 'When they tied ropes to her carriage, so when she started to drive away, graciously waving and bowing farewell to us, she found herself slowly going off backwards, across the lawn. And we had to pretend it was something wrong with the horses, and afterwards she spent hundreds of pounds sending them to the vet to be taught to go forwards again, and couldn't afford to give us any Christmas presents . . .' Which, he admitted, did serve the children right.

'They'll be good this time,' said Mrs Brown. 'Nurse Matilda has made them promise to do exactly as they're told.'

Up in the schoolroom, Ellen was having a difficult time while the children did exactly as they were told all through their lunch. When she said, 'Eat up your plates,' they all began taking great bites out of their plates, and when she said 'Pass the potatoes', they passed the potatoes but not the dish the potatoes were in; and when she said, 'Pass the butter-dish', they passed the dish but not the butter; and when she said (very thankful that the meal was at an end), 'Napkins folded, please!' – they all made a mad rush for the Tiniest Baby which was very happy to find itself suddenly waving its bare pink legs in the air . . . So she went away, rather desperate, only reminding them, 'Now, you are to put your best clothes on.'

'Who shall we *put* them on?' said Simon, when she had gone.

'Or *what* shall we put them on?' said Susie.

'Nobody's told us that,' said Christianna, thoughtfully. 'Ellen just said, "Put your best clothes on—"'

'I shall put mine on the hall table,' said Jaci. 'That'll be a nice welcome for Aunt Adelaide.'

'I shall put mine on the grand piano,' said Helen. 'Its round legs will look sweet in my frilly white drawers.'

'I shall put mine on Sugar,' said Caro, inspired.

'I kook gige og Pike,' said the Baby, before anybody else could.

'I shall put mine on Modestine,' said Susie. Modestine was their terribly grumpy donkey.

'I'll put mine on Aunt Pettitoes,' said Christianna. Aunt Pettitoes was, of course, the old mother sow.

'I'll put mine on Billy Goat,' said Simon.

'—On Nanny Goat,' said Francesca . . .

'We'll put ours on the hens,' said the Littlest Ones, happily. But it was Tora who won.

'I shall put mine on Evangeline,' she said.

'What a lot of noise the animals are making this afternoon,' said Mr and Mrs Brown to one another as they awaited Aunt Adelaide's coming.

The vet had evidently been successful with Aunt Adelaide's horses, for they were pointing the right way and drew her carriage quite uneventfully up to the front door steps. She ascended with great grandeur, pausing only to bend over a perambulator which was standing in the sunshine outside the front door.

'Dear little mite! Thriving splendidly,' said Great Aunt Adelaide, chucking the occupant of the perambulator under its rather beaky chin.

'Cluck, cluck, cluck!' said the occupant of the perambulator, from the depths of starched white embroidery. But after all, that is mostly what the occupants of perambulators do say. And Mr and Mrs Brown did not happen to glance in under the hood.

It was rather surprising to see a heap of white garments neatly folded on the hall table; and that each of the piano's well-turned legs seemed to be wearing a frill of starched white embroidery. But Aunt Adelaide's eyes were Not What they Used to Be – she was getting hard of hearing too – and she seemed to see nothing odd about it. Besides, she was full of a new plan which she now unfolded to Mr and Mrs Brown. She had been thinking things over,

she said, and had come to the conclusion that
Mr and Mrs Brown had too many children –
'Oh, *no*!' cried Mrs Brown – and she had

decided to take one of them, a nice, quiet, well-behaved gel (Aunt Adelaide always called girls 'gels') to live with her; so then they would have at least one less.

Poor Mrs Brown was appalled. Give up one of her dear, darling children to belong to Aunt Adelaide!

'But, Aunt—'

'No argument,' said Aunt Adelaide, raising a large, horny hand. 'I insist. Though no doubt you are overwhelmed by the benefits!' And she outlined the advantages the fortunate child would receive:

Her own suite of rooms, decorated in chocolate brown

A new wardrobe of clothing in colours that wouldn't show the dirt

A pug dog

A canary

A writing-desk

A work-box

And private tuition in
  elocution,
  deportment,
  French,
  German,
  Italian, and, above all, the pianoforte.

'Oh, but none of them could *bear* it!' sobbed Mrs Brown.

'What does she say?' demanded Aunt Adelaide, astounded.

'She says she couldn't bear it,' said Mr Brown, hastily. 'Parting with one of the children, she means.'

'Poof, nonsense!' said Aunt Adelaide. 'One out of so many? You'd never even miss her.'

'Aunt Adelaide you'd – you'd find that – well, that it wouldn't suit you.'

Aunt Adelaide's little rhinoceros eye began to grow red and angry.

'I may find that it doesn't suit me to leave you all my money when I die,' she said grimly. And she banged on the drawing-room carpet with her parasol – quite like Nurse Matilda, only in Aunt Adelaide's case nothing extraordinary happened.

'We shall now take a stroll about your grounds and observe your various daughters in, as it were, their natural habitat; and I shall choose one that appeals to me. I shall then take tea; China tea, if you please, and some thin brown bread and butter. By the time I am ready to leave, the chosen child will be waiting for me in my carriage, with a small bag packed with overnight wear. Otherwise,' said Aunt Adelaide, 'I shall be obliged to reconsider my Will.'

And she marched out with her little rhinoceros eye very beady and her large rhinoceros nose very set and determined; and down the front steps and into the garden. Mr and Mrs Brown followed her and simply didn't know what to do.

The children, meanwhile, had been struggling with the disposal of their best clothes. The hall table and the grand piano had been easy enough; but the pets and the farmyard animals were proving a little more difficult.

In those days, children's clothes were very stiff and starchy and frilly, and best clothes were usually white. The boys wore white sailor suits with round, white sailor caps and black silk scarves, and a whistle on a cord round their necks. The girls wore white embroidered dresses, very frilly, and several white petticoats underneath, very frilly too; and under the frilly white petticoats, frilly white drawers. And on top of the lot they wore frilly, round, white hats. I must say the poor things looked absolutely hideous.

And everything was starched: so starched

that when it came back from the laundry the clothes were all stuck together and made a lovely sort of tearing-apart noise as you put your arm into a sleeve or your leg into a leg.

Sugar and Spice had put up with it fairly good-temperedly, and were now playing happily on the lawn. Mr and Mrs Brown saw them first and they held their breath. Aunt Adelaide peered across the grass at them, with her short-sighted eyes.

'A pretty pair,' she declared at last. 'But you have let them stay out in the sun too much. How dark their limbs appear, against their white clothes! And – can that be a piece of raw meat the little dears are playing with ?'

Mr and Mrs Brown said in faltering accents that they didn't think it could be raw meat that the little dears were playing with – though in fact it was – and hurried Aunt Adelaide on. But their desperate glances said, behind her back, What on *earth* are the children up to now ?

The children had got Aunt Pettitoes dressed at last, and though all her buttons wouldn't do up at the back, she looked very well, standing with her two front feet on the wall of her sty, looking about her and grunting

happily from beneath the rim of her floppy, round, white, embroidered hat.

But Nanny and Billy, the Goats, were being dreadfully difficult, as goats simply always are.

Billy had got Simon's trousers on all right, and the square, white sailor jacket, but Nanny, buttoned tightly into Francesca's dress, had immediately eaten his black silk scarf and then the cord of his whistle; and now by mistake she had swallowed the whistle as well and every time she breathed she went *Wheeeeeeeeee!*

And worst of all was Modestine. She really was a very grumpy donkey and cared for nothing but carrots; and certainly Susie's clothes were on the tight side for her, and the children had had to add some more clothes of the other children's – and Modestine was dreadfully uncomfortable.

The smaller children appeared to Aunt Adelaide, as she made her exploratory progress across the lawn, to be lolloping about in a very aimless fashion, tripping over their white dresses and chattering among themselves with a quite extraordinary mixture of hisses and clucks and bleats and grunts.

'You should bring in an elocution tutor at once,' she said to Mr and Mrs Brown. 'Their diction is disgraceful.' But anyway, they were all too small for her. 'Where are your older gels ?' demanded Aunt Adelaide, beginning to grow a little suspicious that they were not going to be paraded for her to choose from. But, immediately, she caught sight of one of them, standing, quiet and well-behaved; just the sort of little girl she preferred. 'Let us go over and speak to her,' said Aunt Adelaide, waving with her parasol to where Aunt Pettitoes stood sunning herself, proud and pleased, in her white embroidered dress, with her little pink front-hooves propped up on the pigsty wall.

Oh *dear* !

Mr and Mrs Brown looked desperately at one another: there seemed to be no inspiration anywhere. And then – was that a glimpse of rusty black, motionless among the bushes at the edge of the shrubbery? – was that the faintest tinkle of jet, in a black bonnet? At any rate – inspiration came.

'Oh, I don't think she would suit you, Aunt Adelaide,' said Mr Brown, confidently.

'Why not?' asked Aunt Adelaide.

'She snores,' said Mr Brown, without a moment's pause.

'That will not signify. She will have her own suite of rooms. I shall not hear her at night.'

'But she snores all day too,' said Mrs Brown, just as inspired as Mr Brown; and certainly some very curious noises were coming from under the floppy white hat.

'Oh. Well, that's different,' said Aunt Adelaide, balked. She stopped in her tracks and stood looking about her: sniffing the air like a pointer scenting further prey. 'What is that curious whistling noise?'

The whistling noise was Nanny Goat, who now appeared galloping wildly round the corner from the stables, looking very odd indeed, it must be confessed, with her frilly hat caught up on one horn and her knickers coming down. And just when the Browns were praying that she would continue her mad career, she did just what goats always do – which is the thing you don't want them to do – and came to a sudden stop with all her four hooves bunched together, slap in front of Great-Aunt Adelaide; and stood there gazing up earnestly into her face. 'And which little gel are *you*?' said Aunt Adelaide, evidently rather taken by this flattering behaviour.

'Wheeeeeeeeeeeee!' went Nanny Goat.

'Severe asthma!' said Mr Brown, hurriedly. 'You wouldn't want—'

'I shall call in the Best Doctors,' said Aunt Adelaide. She gave Nanny a poke with her parasol. 'Stand up straight, dear, and answer properly when spoken to.'

In the ordinary way, Nanny Goat would, upon this, have taken to her heels and fled off across the grass; but of course she must do the wrong thing as usual, and to the horror of the Browns she got up on her hind legs, as ordered, and remained, as before, gazing earnestly into the old lady's face. The Browns stood paralysed, and prayed to hear once again that tiny, magic tinkle of jet.

Aunt Adelaide remained for one terrible moment gazing back at Nanny Goat. Then she gave her a second prod with the parasol and this time Nanny did take the hint.

'Poor child,' said Aunt Adelaide, watching her as she dashed off, tripping at every other step over the coming-down drawers. And she shuddered over the memory of it. 'Too sad, my dears! The little beard,' she said, shaking her head.

'Who is that Person?' asked Aunt Adelaide next, suddenly pointing with her parasol.

'What person?' asked Mr and Mrs Brown. They couldn't see anyone at all.

'An ill-favoured female, standing over there, in rusty black, with jet in her bonnet and a nose like two potatoes.'

'Whoever can it be?' said Mrs Brown. 'Has she got a Tooth?'

'Yes, a Tooth,' said Aunt Adelaide. 'And a large black stick.'

'Oh, it must be Nurse Matilda,' said Mrs Brown. 'How early she has come back from her day off!' But *she* couldn't see Nurse Matilda and neither could Mr Brown. 'Perhaps,' she said, 'she has gone round behind the stables.'

From behind the stables came a terrible

'Hee-haaaaaaw! Hee-haaaaaaaaaaaaw! Hee-haaaaaaaaaaaaw!'

The children had got Modestine dressed at last, but they had to admit that she looked very odd. It had taken the best clothes of three of the girls to cover her, and even then her tail hung out at the back. Still, they had a floppy hat over each ear, and if only she'd kept her mouth shut, she'd have done very well. But she didn't. No longer able to kick out at them – for her legs were tightly buttoned into a petticoat apiece – she kept up her continuous, terrible braying; and now she had broken away from them and they knew that in half a minute she would be round the stables and out on the lawn in front of their advancing Mama and Papa and their Great-Aunt Adelaide; and though they didn't know about Aunt Adelaide wanting one of them to take home with her, they did know about her leaving all her money to Papa and Mama when she died, and that she wouldn't if she was upset. And a chicken, two dachshunds, several geese, a pig and a goat, all dressed in starched white frillies, might so far have failed to upset Great-Aunt Adelaide; but they knew that Modestine and her dreadful hee-hawing was going too far. 'Oh, dear,' they said, 'if only Nurse Matilda were here!'

And suddenly – there she was! – black, trembly bonnet, nose, Tooth, stick and all.

'Why – what do you think *I* would do for you, you naughty children?' said Nurse Matilda; and she bit her lip and looked terribly stern.

'You might bang with your stick—?' suggested the children, hanging on to Modestine for dear life.

'That usually makes things worse,' said Nurse Matilda. 'Doesn't it?'

'Yes, it does,' said the children; and they looked unhappily at Nurse Matilda. And then they looked at her again. Was it possible – was it just possible that Nurse Matilda was biting her lip to keep herself from laughing?

'Well – we'll try,' said Nurse Matilda. And she added, 'But not for your sakes, you naughty children! For your Papa's sake and Mama's.' And she banged with her big black stick on the stable floor.

But too late! At that moment Modestine broke away from their clutching hands and shot round the corner of the stable, floppy hats, starchy dresses, frilly petticoats and all – and, hee-hawing like a lunatic, dashed across the lawn, with all the children streaming after her, slap in front of Great-Aunt Adelaide. Great-Aunt Adelaide turned upon Mr and Mrs Brown with a face of outraged horror, her parasol raised in one gloved hand, the very figure of doom . . .

And in that second, Nurse Matilda's black stick once again came down on the stable floor; and Aunt Adelaide lowered her parasol, and to the amazement of Mr and Mrs Brown, there spread over her enraged features a smile which really was almost idiotic in its rapture.

'Why, what a merry game!' cried Aunt Adelaide, as Modestine swerved and went galloping across the grass, all the children in panic-chase behind her. 'What a charming-looking gel! See how prettily she sports with the lads and lassies from the village – rough and ill-clad though they be! Hear her joyous laughter!' ('Hee-haw! Hee-haw!' went Modestine.) 'See! – now she dodges behind a bush! Now she has turned and pretends to run after *them* – how they all flee from her!' And she clasped her horny old hands in an ecstasy of delight, and turned upon Mr and Mrs Brown. 'This is the gel for me! I have not seen such

spirit, such light-heartedness for many a long day. We can do with some of her gaiety at Stitch Hall.' And she clapped her hands and called out in silvery accents: 'Come here, dear! Come to me!'

'Hee-haw! Hee-haw!' went Modestine, galloping angrily after the children and nipping them sharply in the backs of their legs.

'She does not hear me. Come, dear!' called Aunt Adelaide, winningly. 'What is her name?' she said to Mrs Brown.

'Her – her name is Modestine,' said Mrs Brown.

'Come, Modestine!' called Aunt Adelaide.

'But I'm afraid she is really a – a donkey,' said Mr Brown.

'Nonsense,' said Aunt Adelaide, sharply. 'Just because the gel revels in a childish game, don't start calling her names . . .' But she was growing a little tired herself of the childish game. 'Bring her to me,' she said, imperiously. 'I have decided. This is the gel I shall choose!'

'But Aunt Adelaide—' began Mr Brown.

'But Aunt Adelaide—' cried Mrs Brown.

'No argument. If,' said Aunt Adelaide, 'Modestine is not in my carriage, bag packed and ready to depart, by the time I have had my cup of tea – not a penny piece of mine shall you ever see.' And she added: 'There is that Person again.'

And this time they did see her – Nurse Matilda, walking across the lawn towards them, still in her bonnet and rusty black jacket, as though she had only just that minute got back from her day off.

'Good evening, Madam,' she said, making a little bob in the direction of Aunt Adelaide; and to Mrs Brown she said: 'I am just this minute back from my day off. Is there anything I can do for you?'

'I am taking your Miss Modestine home with me,' said Aunt Adelaide, not letting Mrs Brown reply. 'I wish her to be ready, bag packed, and waiting in my carriage in a quarter of an hour from now.'

'Very well, Madam,' said Nurse Matilda; and she made a little bob again and went quietly away. Aunt Adelaide turned and hurried happily back to the front door.

A great quiet had fallen over house and garden. Dazed and apprehensive, not knowing what would happen, Mrs Brown poured out China tea for Great-Aunt Adelaide and pressed on her the brown bread and butter. Aunt Adelaide ate very little. She was far too excited and happy, reminding the bewildered Mr and Mrs Brown with her plans for dear Modestine's future:

'A suite of rooms, my dears, decorated in chocolate brown

A whole new wardrobe of clothes in dark colours so as not to show the dirt

A pug dog

A canary

A writing-desk

A work-box

And private tuition in

   elocution,

   deportment,

   French,

   German,

   Italian, and, above all, the pianoforte . . .

'And when she is of age,' concluded Aunt Adelaide, 'I shall single out a suitable young man for her to marry—' ('He will be an ass!' said Mr Brown under his breath, making a sort of awful joke of it, to try to cheer himself up.) '—I know the very young man, Adolphus Haversack, grandson of an old friend of mine. You need not fear for your legacy, my dears,' added Aunt Adelaide, seeing their anxious faces – which, however, were anxious for a very different reason: for how would they ever get Modestine into the carriage? 'She shall marry so well, that she'll need no money from me. It shall all come to you, for the happiness you have given me in allowing me to take away this dear gel of yours.' And she looked out of the window and cried: 'Ah, there she is! Ready and waiting.'

And there she was – ready and waiting: sitting up in the carriage, not hee-hawing at all, simply sitting still, looking down modestly into her lap. Nurse Matilda stood respectfully by, with the little case of night-things all beautifully packed, in her hand.

Mr and Mrs Brown, standing wretchedly on the front steps as Great-Aunt Adelaide gaily mounted up into the carriage, looked distrustfully at Nurse Matilda. Could it be possible that this had been her way of helping? – that instead of urging Modestine into the carriage, she had sent off one of their own dear children? They tried to peer under the floppy white hat, but Modestine still hung her head – shedding a tear, perhaps, over the home she was leaving, for all the glories of the chocolate-coloured rooms and the lessons on the piano-forte? And – horror of horrors! – from the far-away stables came a sound that surely was 'Hee-haw! Hee-haw!' 'Aunt Adelaide—!' cried Mrs Brown, not able to bear the suspense one moment longer . . . But too late! Clip, clop, clip, clop, went the horses' hooves: and the carriage had turned the corner of the drive and was out of sight.

'Nurse Matilda,' cried Mr and Mrs Brown, terrified, 'which of them—?'

From the stables came, 'Hee-haw; hee-haaaaaaaaaw . . .'

'Now then, Modestine,' Aunt Adelaide was saying, in the carriage. 'Look up and smile. I am sure you are going to be happy.'

'Oh, I'm sure I am,' said Modestine, looking up and smiling all over her face. 'Only—'

'Your own suite of rooms, Modestine; decorated throughout in chocolate brown . . .'

'Oh, thank you, how lovely!' said Modestine. 'Only—'

'A new wardrobe of dresses in dark colours so as not to show the dirt . . .'

'Oh, thank you,' said Modestine. 'Only—'

'And a pug dog—
And a canary—
And a writing-desk—
And a work-box—'

'How *lovely*,' said Modestine. 'Only—'

'—and private tuition in
elocution,
deportment,
French,
German,
Italian,
and,
above all,
the pianoforte . . .'

'Oh, thank you, Ma'am,' said Modestine, respectfully. 'Only—'

'You may call me Great-Aunt Adelaide,' said Great-Aunt Adelaide, graciously. And she added: 'Only – what?'

'Only you have my name a little wrong,

Great-Aunt Adelaide. It's not *Modest*ine: it's *Evange*line.'

And so everyone was made happy. Great-Aunt Adelaide was happy because she had one of Mr and Mrs Brown's family (as she thought). And Evangeline was happy because she had the chocolate-coloured rooms and beautiful new dresses and the pug dog and the canary and the writing-desk and the work-box and all that private tuition. And Mrs Brown was happy because, although Aunt Adelaide had one of her children and was happy, she hadn't really got one of them, but she was still happy. And Mr Brown was very, very happy because he and his family would still have all Great-Aunt Adelaide's money when she died; which, however, he did most sincerely hope wouldn't be for many years to come, and, in fact, it wasn't – for Great-Aunt Adelaide lived to see Evangeline, beautiful and talented, united with that very Adolphus Haversack whom she had mentioned to Mr and Mrs Brown. And the Staff were happy for Evangeline's sake, who, however much put upon, had always been such a cheerful little lump; and they soon got another tweeny-maid and put upon her instead.

And night fell, and bedtime came: and Mrs Brown stood with Nurse Matilda at the nursery door.

'But why aren't the children asleep?' she said.

'Well, they are,' said Nurse Matilda.

'They're not in their beds?' said Mrs Brown.

'They're in the beds they have chosen,' said Nurse Matilda; and she smiled her own smile at Mrs Brown and said, softly: 'Lesson Six is almost over. Lesson Seven is about to begin.'

Chapter 9

WHERE Modestine – the real Modestine – slept that night, I don't know; though, no doubt, in her mysterious way, Nurse Matilda saw to it that she was comfortable – as comfortable as Aunt Pettitoes and Nanny Goat and Billy Goat and Sugar and Spice and the lambs and the geese and the hens. But where the children slept, I *can* tell you – for Susie slept in the stable, and Caro and the Baby slept curled up in the dog-basket, and Francesca and Simon slept in the goat pen, and some of the children slept among the geese, and some of them slept with the lambs, and the Littlest Ones nid-nodded on perches in the hen-house . . . Poor Christianna was the worst off – but, after all, nobody had *asked* her to change clothes with Aunt Pettitoes, had they?

And nobody had asked the other children to change with Modestine and the dogs and the goats and the geese and the hens.

But they had: and this was still Lesson Six.

I suppose it was because they were so uncomfortable that the children, that night, began to dream. At least it was a sort of dream. Afterwards they were never quite sure how much of it had been a dream and how much had been real. The dream was that at last – very, very early in the morning, almost before the sun was up – they all got up and went and met the others under the big beech tree on the lawn and said: 'This is too much. Let's run away.' And that suddenly, before they knew how it had happened, they *were* running away.

They couldn't stop it.

The house was very quiet. As they began to run, jogging across the lawn towards the drive and the big front gate, the windows seemed to frown down upon them, disapprovingly – those tall first-floor windows where, so long ago, they had mopped and mowed to frighten away the new nanny and nurses and the new governess, and the skinny little nursery-maid. They wished the house didn't seem so cross with them, standing there, frowning and silent, in the first faint light of the dawn, as though it were angry with them for wanting to leave it – for wanting to run away. But, in fact, they *didn't* want to run away. They'd run away often enough before, not caring two pins what the old house thought, never even considering that it might feel insulted and hurt, to be run away from; but this time it wasn't their fault – they didn't *want* to go.

And, what was more, they decided, suddenly, they weren't going to go, either – they were going to run back, they were going to run up the front steps and in at the front door and up to their own warm beds and never run away again . . .

They couldn't stop running, but they wheeled in their tracks and went back up the drive and up the front steps and pushed at the big front door.

It wouldn't open.

The door – their own, dear, old, welcoming, front door – it wouldn't open for them. And they couldn't stop – they had to keep on running. They ran down the steps again and down the drive; and as they ran, they thought: Perhaps the gate won't open either – and then we can't run away. We'll be safe. We'll just keep running round the garden till the grown-ups wake up and come down and stop us . . .

But, just as the front door wouldn't open – the gate wouldn't keep shut. As they approached it, it swung gently open, and – they couldn't help it, they couldn't stop – out they ran, and into the village street. And now they were really running away and there was nothing to be done about it but just to keep on.

They ran and they ran. The Big Ones ran first, the Littler Ones trailed after them, the Littlest Ones trailed after *them* – and last of all, the poor Baby, stumping along on its little bandy legs, as determined as ever not to be left behind. And all about them the village slept, the friendly doors of the little shops were shut, the closed eyes of the windows would not look at them as they passed. They came to the police-station and thought they saw the shadow of Constable Figgs on the blind (for we know

that the Force Never Sleeps), and they called
out, 'Constable Figgs, please come out and
stop us!' but nothing happened and they
called even louder, 'Come and stop us, arrest
us, we've eaten up Podge Green!' If they were
arrested, they thought, and thrown into
prison, then they'd *have* to stop running; and
soon their mother and father would come and
bail them out.

But just as it seemed to them that the constable's shadow on the blind began to turn,

as though he had heard and would do something about it, a window was slammed up and Podge Green's fat, round face appeared and he cried out, 'No, they haven't eaten me! I wasn't a Balanced Meal!' and the window slammed down again, and the shadow on the blind didn't move any more; and the children ran on.

They ran on and on, and as they ran their feet went squildge, squildge, squildge in their boots: and they looked down, and all of a sudden it seemed to them in this strange half-dream that they had Wellington boots on – and the boots were full of treacle. So they tried to ease the boots off as they ran, but it was no use because they had great big woolly grey socks on, too, and the socks had been dipped in porridge and the mixture of porridge and treacle was simply awful. And they had their best clothes on, the boys in white sailor suits and round sailor caps, and the girls in their white embroidered dresses and frilly round white hats. The starch scratched and prickled as they ran, and the girls' hats fell down over their eyes, and they couldn't see where they were going. It didn't matter because they just had to keep running, anyway.

And beneath the sailor caps and the round, white hats, their poor faces were covered with large, round, painted spots; and they mopped and mowed as they ran. Sugar and Spice ran behind them, very gaily, dressed in brown Holland smocks and round, grey felt hats. The Baby, with its nappy coming down as usual, struggled along as best it could.

Out of the village, and into the country. The sun had not yet come up and it was grey and chilly in the flower-fresh, empty lanes. We shall run for ever, they thought. There'll be nobody here to stop us. But at that very minute they turned a corner and there, ahead of them, was – of all things! – a four-wheeler cab.

'Help, help!' cried the children. 'Stop us running! Stop us!'

'Yes, yes,' cried a voice from the cab, and a skinny little figure hopped out and came running towards them.

Help at last!

The skinny little figure ran towards them and they saw that it was a nursery-maid: you could tell she was a nursery-maid because she was so remarkably skinny. And if anyone would rescue them, *she* would. The skinny little nursery-maids were just as much put upon by the nannies and governesses and the starchy nurses as the tweeny-maids were by the Staff; but the children had always been friends with their nursery-maids.

'Oh, Sukey – Maria – Matilda – Mary-Ann,' cried the children, working backwards through all the long succession of nursery-maids. 'Oh, Maggie, Mary-Ann (again), Jemima, Jane – rescue us, save us, we want to stop running away . . . !' And they held out beseeching hands.

The skinny little nursery-maid stopped: stared: gave one startled squeak: and turned and ran back to the cab as fast as her skinny legs would carry her. Eight arms came out like an octopus and dragged her in.

'They're mad,' cried the skinny little nursery-maid. 'They're mopping and mowing! They're mad, and if they bite us we'll go mad too!'

Five alarmed faces gazed out of the back window as the cab galloped wildly away. Sighing sadly, the children ran on; and mopped and mowed as they ran.

The dawn came and still they were running. Justin had both feet in one trouser leg, poor boy, and was hopping along like a robin, Tora had sold all her legs and arms and the Baby was staggering about among the children as they loped along, holding out the little nursery potty and calling, 'Alms for ge luvvy Aggy!' – trying to collect enough to buy them back for her. And every child had a stitch by now, and cried out as it ran, 'Ow my *stitch*!'

'Stitch?' cried a great voice, high and hooting, booming back. 'Who calls for Adelaide Stitch?'

'Aunt Adelaide,' cried the children. 'Save us! Save us!'

Great-Aunt Adelaide Stitch appeared round a corner. She had Evangeline on one side of her, dressed up very finely in dark clothes, not to show the dirt; and on the other a tall young man with large brown eyes, wearing a tight checked suit and curly bowler of the utmost expensiveness.

'This is Adolphus Haversack,' said Aunt Adelaide. 'Dear Evangeline's intended.'

'Oh, Adolphus Haversack,' cried the children, checking their headlong rush, but still having to jog up and down, running on the spot, 'please save us!'

'If anyone can do so,' said Aunt Adelaide, 'it will be Adolphus. He is Exceedingly Rich.'

Adolphus Haversack took off his curly bowler and bowed deeply. 'Anything Miss Evangeline commands,' he said in a voice of silver – everything about Adolphus Haversack was expensive, even his voice – 'anything Miss Evangeline commands, I will do.'

'Evangeline,' cried Great-Aunt Adelaide Stitch, imperiously. 'Command him!'

'Hee-haw,' said Evangeline.

'Hee-haw?' said Adolphus Haversack, startled and surprised.

'Hee-haw,' said Evangeline.

'Come, Evangeline,' said Aunt Adelaide. 'Don't be a little donkey, dear. Talk horse sense.'

'Hee-haw,' said Evangeline.

The children, marking time, jerked up and down and gazed imploringly at Evangeline. Poor Justin was still hopping. Tora had bought back one leg and both of her arms, thanks to the efforts of the Baby, and though somewhat lop-sided, was managing better.

'Evangeline,' they begged. 'Do please command him!'

Evangeline shook her head and her ears rattled. 'Evangeline,' insisted the children, 'if you'll only ask him—'

'—they will give you—' said Aunt Adelaide.

'—a pug dog,' cried the children, jogging up and down anxiously.

'And a canary,' said Aunt Adelaide.

'Yes, and a writing-desk—'

'—and a work-box.'

'Oh, yes and a work-box. And private tuition in—'

'—elocution—' said Aunt Adelaide.

'—and deportment—'

'—and French, German and Italian—'

'—and, above all,' promised the children—
'—lessons in the pianoforte,' finished Aunt
Adelaide triumphantly. 'There, Evangeline –
what do you think of that?'

'Hee-haaaaaaaaaw,' said Evangeline; and
she kicked up her heels and bolted. Aunt
Adelaide Stitch picked up her long skirts and

bolted after her. Adolphus Haversack twirled
his stick and followed them languidly. The
children's feet stopped marking time and
started to run again.

On and on and on.

The sun came up and dried the sparkly dew
on the hedgerows, and breakfast time came
and went, and they were hungry and thirsty,
but there was nothing to eat or drink, and no
time to stop, if there had been, to eat and drink
it. At mid-morning, they thought they smelt
lovely, steaming cocoa; but it was only a little

stream running under a bridge, and the cocoa was made with mud. And when dinner-time came, they caught a whiff of steak-and-kidney pudding and, sure enough, there it was, great platefuls of it spread out on a table by the wayside, with a great dish of golden roly-poly beside it. But as, streaming by, they reached out their hungry hands to grab some, a huge cardboard notice came down like a guillotine between the plates and their hands, saying GOING TO WASTE ON ACCOUNT OF MEASLES. From behind the bushes, as they ran, came a chorus of throaty giggling, and out between the roots of the hedgerows poked little, jeering, sausage faces, and they saw, now, that the flowers in the hedgerows weren't flowers at all, really, but dabs and blobs of white blancmange and pink jelly. They'd have welcomed even jelly and blancmange by now, but they couldn't stop to pick any – they had to keep on running.

The long day passed – the long, long, weary day. At tea-time, they thought they saw a gleam of silver up on the hillside, where a tiny river started off on its life's journey; but it was tea, really, pouring down the hillside from a huge brown nursery teapot, and just as they came up to it, gasping, there was another huge brown teapot by the roadside, and the tea all flowed back into it and disappeared, and the lid went on with a *clop*! and they couldn't stop to get it off. 'We can't run any more,' said the poor children, desperately. 'We can't!' But they had to. They just couldn't not run.

Evening came. They breasted the top of a hill and saw Aunt Pettitoes sunning herself there in the dying light, her front hooves elegantly crossed as she leaned on a low wall.

'Look, dears,' said Aunt Pettitoes to her piglets as the children trailed past her, 'there are the children, running away!'

'Aunt Pettitoes, stop us, save us,' cried the children. 'We don't *want* to be running away.'

'Pooh, nonsense,' said Aunt Pettitoes. 'I know you children – you're always running away.'

'You're unkind and horrid and your babies look like vegetable marrows,' cried the children, resentfully, 'and you look jolly silly yourself, in that frilly round hat.'

But they still had to keep on running. They passed Billy and Nanny, and a gaggle of geese, and their friends the speckled hens: but the goats and the geese and the hens were all busy trying on sailor suits and frilly dresses and took no notice of a long file of children wearily jog-trotting by.

And then, suddenly – hope again! They seemed to have run all day between nothing but deserted country lanes. But now there was a village in sight.

Weary, failing, hungry and thirsty, on tottering legs the children streeled into the village, strung out in a straggling line – the Big Ones leading, plodding doggedly on, the Middlings trailing behind them, the Little Ones stumbling after *them*, dragging the Littlest ones by small, hot, unwilling hands: the Baby still gamely staggering along at the very end, with its nappy round its fat, bent knees. Sugar and Spice still frisked at their heels, wearing the Holland smocks and the round grey hats. (*They* weren't being taught any lesson, they were only little dogs: someone – Someone – was seeing to it that Sugar and Spice didn't feel or suffer as the naughty children must.)

The curtains were drawn in the little village street, the lamps were beginning to be lit. For dusk had fallen. The children had been running the whole day long.

Wearily, wearily they jog-trotted into the lamp-lit street.

'Save us!' they cried to the curtained windows, where the warm lights glowed.

'Of course!' cried a hundred voices from within. 'Of course we will!'

Squeaky voices, growly voices, ol'-man-river voices: short, sharp, barking-out-orders voices . . . Dolls' voices, teddy bears' voices, golliwogs' voices, the voices of tin soldiers . . . The voices of the children's toys!

'We're safe at last, cried the children. 'The toys will rescue us.'

And the curtains parted and windows slammed up and the toys poked out their heads . . .

And chop, chop, chop! – a scatter of wax, of sawdust, of cotton-wool stuffing, of broken lead – and the heads fell plop, plop, plop! into the village street.

The toys would have rescued the children; but long ago Nicolas had executed them all.

And so, despair in their hearts, the children ran on.

But now . . . It was a very strange village. For now the main street ended suddenly – in a huge, big, green Baize Door.

They needn't go any farther. They just couldn't. They wouldn't be *able* to run any more. The Baize Door barred their way.

And here were Hoppitt and Cook and Celeste and Alice and Emily standing before the Baize Door; and crying out with one voice, 'Lawks a mussy! – who's this?'

'Oh, Hoppitt! Oh, Cook!' cried the children, faint with thankfulness. 'It's the children. It's *us*!'

At least, that's what they meant to say. But what do you think came out? 'Oh, Humps mumps! Oh, Cumps! Dumps the Chumps mumps! Dumps *umps*!'

'Foreigners!' cried Hoppitt, and flung wide the door and stood aside: and slowly, wearily, but inexorably, the children's legs began to carry them through and out on the road again. 'Stop us! Stop us!' cried the children, desperately, clutching at the last straw. But it came out as 'Stumps umps!' and Hoppitt only added, 'Foreign cricketers at that; we don't want the likes of them here,' and flattened himself against the open Baize Door to let them pass.

'They look tired, poor things,' said kind Alice and Emily, and bent to peer into their faces. 'And all them spots!' they added, pitifully.

'Spots?' shrieked Celeste.

'Fetch the medicine,' cried Cook.

'Fetch the brooms, you mean,' screamed Celeste. 'Fetch the mops, fetch my curling tongs. It's the Measles. We don't want the Measles here!'

And nip, nip, nip went the curling tongs, and swish went the brooms and bang went the mops; and the children were through the door and out on the long, chill, darkling road again; and the stars came out and it was night. And they ran and they ran . . .

And suddenly – the Baby fell down. It tripped over its nappy at last, and stumbled and fell; and it sat in a round, mournful bundle in the middle of the road and just couldn't get up. And at last put its fat round fists in its eyes and sobbed out: 'Nurk Magiggy. Wonk Nurk Magiggy! Wairg my Nurk Magiggy?'

And a voice said out of the darkness, and as velvet as the darkness, 'Darling Baby: I am here.' And out of the darkness came two arms and caught up the Baby against a loving shoulder and held it close.

And all the children stopped running at that moment and cried out, 'Oh, why didn't we think of it before? Nurse Matilda — come to us!'

And the voice said: 'Yes, children. Yes, darlings. I am here.'

And in that one moment — how could it have happened that to each child it seemed as if those loving arms came around him and he was lifted up gently and his weary head cradled against a kind shoulder? And he was carried softly and silently through the night and slipped into his own warm, cosy bed at home: washed and brushed and changed into pyjamas, teeth cleaned, prayers said and peacefully dreaming . . .

Dreaming that he was running away: but would wake up in his bed in the morning, all safe and sound — only quite, quite certain never to run away again.

For that had been Lesson Seven.

Chapter 10

THAT afternoon Mrs Brown said to Nurse Matilda, 'It is too dreadful, but a friend of mine called Mrs Black is coming this afternoon, and she will want to see the children.'

So Nurse Matilda said to the children, 'A friend of your Mama's, called Mrs Black, is coming this afternoon and will wish to see you. Wash your hands and faces and put on your best clothes and go down to the drawing-room.' And she lifted her big black stick as though she were about to give one thump on the floor with it; and changed her mind and just added calmly, 'Please, children.'

So the children went upstairs and washed their hands and faces and put on their best clothes and went down to the drawing-room and sat down quietly in a ring all round their

Mama and Mrs Black. And Mrs Black said, 'I never *saw* such well-behaved children.'

'Aren't they?' said Mrs Brown, beaming. She had never for one moment really thought her children were naughty.

'When I left home,' said Mrs Black, 'this is what *my* children were doing:

Emma had put a piglet in the baby's cot and sent for the doctor.

Lucy'd filled the loo with sticks and coal and lit a fire in it.

Thomas had tied the twins' plaits together behind their heads, and they couldn't get apart.

Victoria had covered little William with squished-up tomatoes to be a Red Indian, and put on his clothes on top of it.

And all my other children were doing simply dreadful things too.'

And Mrs Brown and all the children said with one voice, 'The person *you* need is Nurse Matilda.'

And then the children added, very quickly: 'Only you can't have her. She's ours.'

Nurse Matilda stood in the doorway and she smiled. She smiled and she smiled – but yet, at the same time, two big tears gathered in her eyes and rolled down her cheeks. And as they rolled – they seemed to roll away the very last of Nurse Matilda's wrinkles. And her face wasn't round and brown any more, and her nose, like two potatoes, was changing its shape altogether: and even her rusty black clothes seemed to be getting all goldeny. And when Mrs Black whispered to Mrs Brown, 'But she's so *ugly*!' Mrs Brown whispered back in astonishment, 'How can you say so? She's perfectly lovely!'

But Nurse Matilda's two tears rolled on down her face; and she said to Mrs Brown, 'I told you.'

'Told me what?' said Mrs Brown; and all the children cried out, 'Told her what?' and then corrected themselves and asked politely, 'Please tell us what it was you told Mama.'

And Nurse Matilda said, 'I told her that when you didn't need me – but you did want me: then I must leave you.' And all the children burst out crying and said, 'Oh, no, don't leave us – don't leave us . . . !'

And Nurse Matilda smiled through her tears and said, 'I don't want to – I've loved you all so much, you really have been far, far the naughtiest of *all* my children . . .' And her smile was so lovely that she would have looked

like the loveliest person in all the world if only
– well, even the children and Mrs Brown had
to admit it – if only it hadn't been for that
terrible Tooth! And at that moment, just as
they were thinking it – couldn't *help* thinking
it – she gave one last thump with her stick on
the ground and – what do you think happened ?
That Tooth of hers flew out, and landed on the
floor at the children's feet.

And it began to grow.

It grew and it grew. It grew until it was
the size of a match-box. It grew until it
was the size of a snuff-box. It grew until it was
the size of a shoe-box – of a tuck-box – of a suit-
case – of a packing-case – of a trunk: of a big
trunk, a huge trunk, a simply enormous trunk.

. . . And suddenly the trunk flew open and, inside, it was crammed to the top, full up, bursting, bulging out at the seams with toys – the most marvellous toys you ever saw. And the more toys they took out of it, the more toys seemed to remain to be taken out: not one toy for each child, not two toys for each child, but dozens and dozens of wonderful toys for every single child in the whole Brown family. . . .

When they all had their toys and at last the trunk was empty and they looked up again – Nurse Matilda was gone.